The Earth Shook
A PERSIAN TALE

DONNA JO NAPOLI

Illustrations by

GABI SWIATKOWSKA

Disney · HYPERION BOOKS
New York

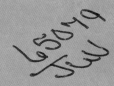

Printed in Singapore

First Edition   1 3 5 7 9 10 8 6 4 2

Library of Congress Cataloging-in-Publication Data on file.

ISBN 978-1-4231-0448-3

Reinforced binding

Visit www.hyperionbooksforchildren.com

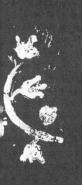
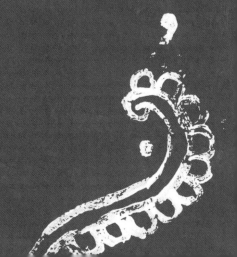

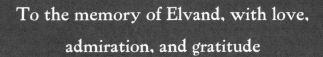

To the memory of Elvand, with love,
admiration, and gratitude

— D J N

For Sophie, the queen of Puymirol

— G S

Good night, my angel. Sleep safe from the danger outside the town walls.

The earth shook.
Parisa fell from her bed and tumbled out the door.
Homes collapsed.

No one was left within the town walls except Parisa.

She slipped outside like a frightened whisper.

Saturday she knocked on a door.

Boar answered.
"Hands like grasping vines, you remind me of a hunter who
threw spears at me. See these tusks?
Run, or I'll gore a hole through you."

Sunday she knocked on a door.

Snapping Turtle answered.
"Pincer hands, you remind me of a scorpion who tried to sting me to death.
Run, or I'll drown you in the river."

Parisa decided to glove her hands.

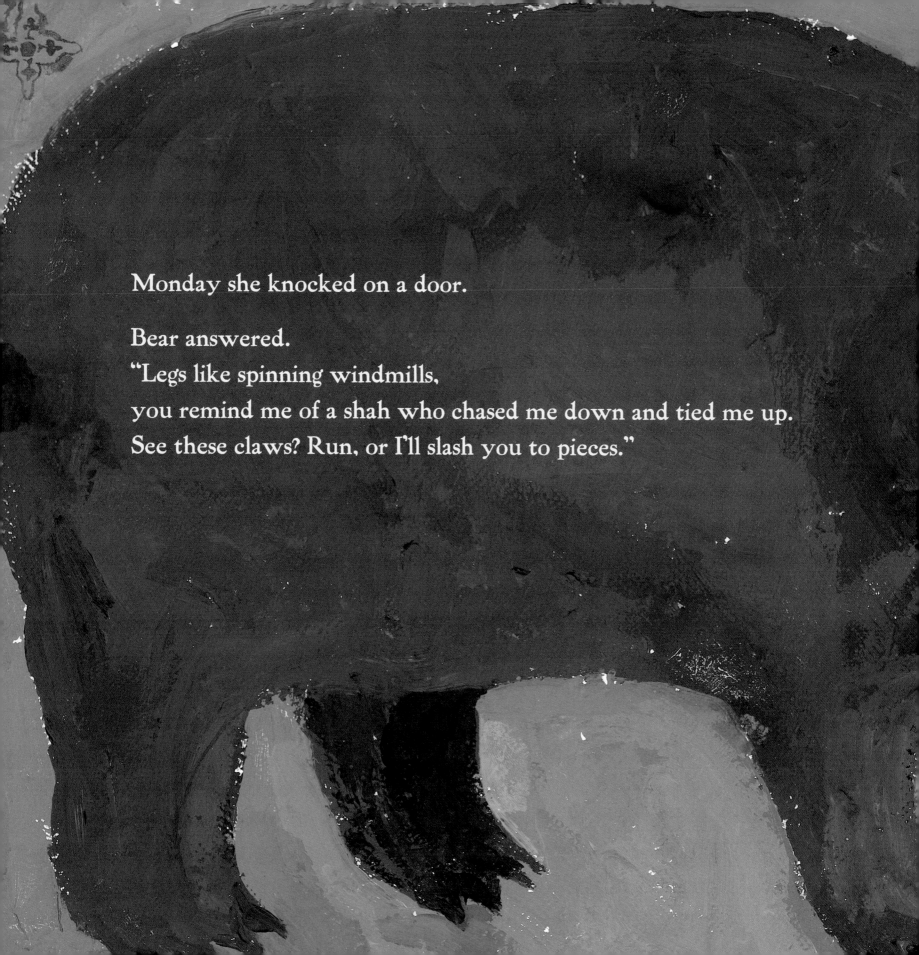

Monday she knocked on a door.

Bear answered.
"Legs like spinning windmills,
you remind me of a shah who chased me down and tied me up.
See these claws? Run, or I'll slash you to pieces."

Tuesday she knocked on a door.

Owl answered.
"Big hind legs, you
remind me of a rabbit who
hopped away and left me starving.
Run, or I'll rip you to shreds."

Parisa decided to cover her legs.

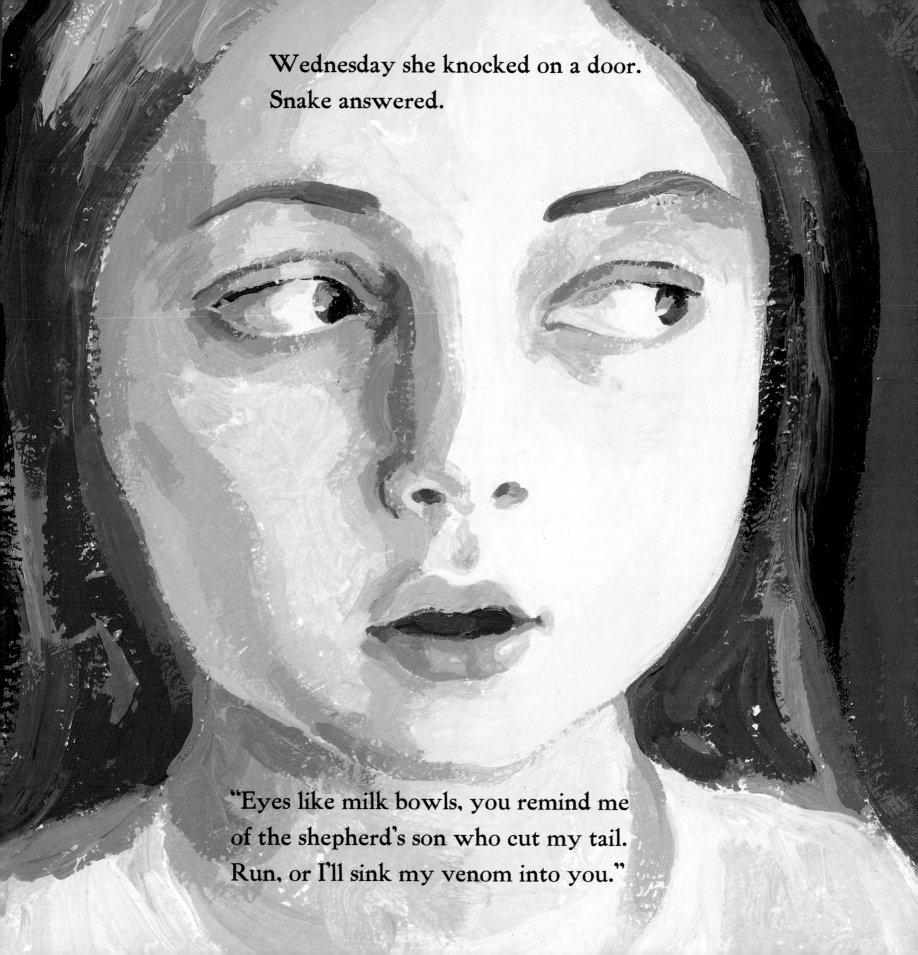

Wednesday she knocked on a door.
Snake answered.

"Eyes like milk bowls, you remind me
of the shepherd's son who cut my tail.
Run, or I'll sink my venom into you."

Thursday she knocked on a door.

Wolf answered.

"Black Eyes, you remind me of the tattletale goat whose brothers I ate. Run, or I'll eat you too."

Parisa decided to veil her eyes.

Friday she knocked on a door.

Lion answered.

"ROARRRRRRRR!"

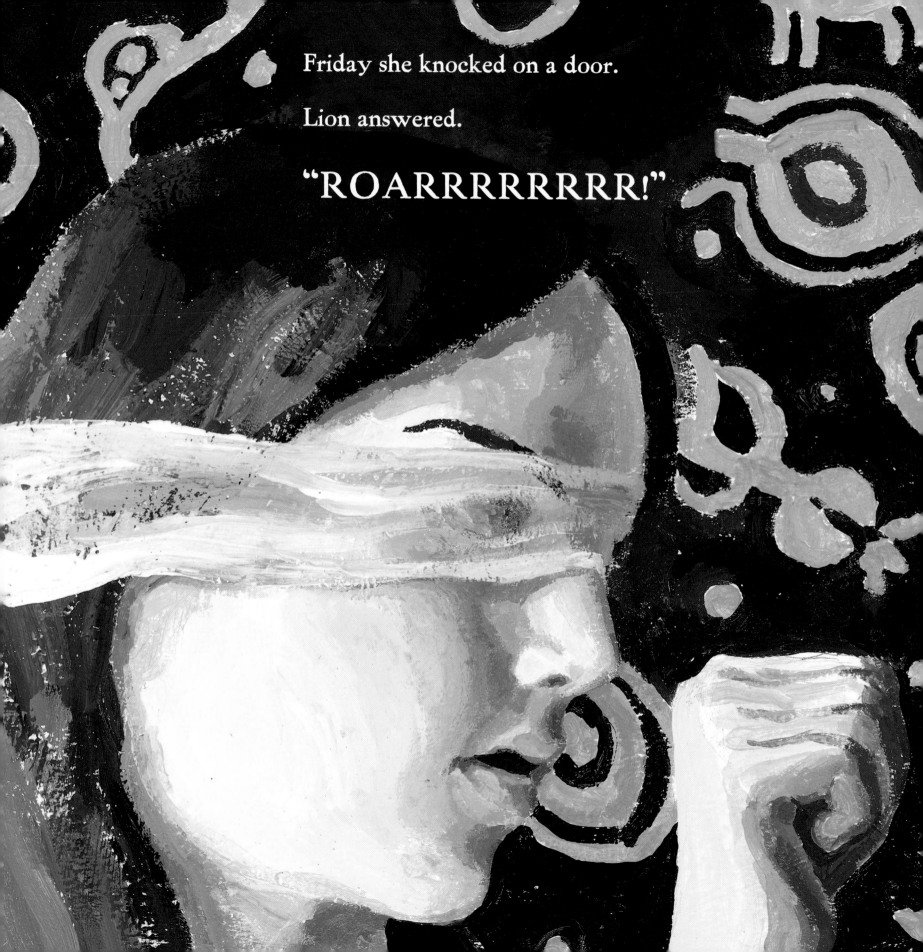

Parisa stood alone in the sun.

She sat on her heels and lowered her forehead to the sand.
"I'm sick and tired of monsters.
I'm looking for a human being."

But she saw no human beings
except herself.

"Well, then, I'll just be with myself.
And do what humans do."

She took off her veil and her gloves and the
covering on her legs. Now anyone could see
Parisa's light was human, and not the moon at sunset,
or the stars at night. She walked as a human child
under the sun.

"Nobody's thinking of the flowers," said Parisa to herself.
"Human beings think of flowers."
She dug a pool till water filled it from below.
She watered the thirsty flowers.

Boar's tusks were perfect for digging.
He dug another pool beside the first.

Snapping Turtle basked in it.

"Bits of dust dance and embrace the sun,"
said Parisa to herself.
"Human beings are not less."

She made a drum and danced.

Bear's paws were perfect for beating on the earth.
He padded this way and that.

Owl bobbed on a branch,
hooting in rhythm.

"The mountaintop greets the snow, new snow, with a laugh," said Parisa to herself. "Human beings need to laugh."
She told herself joke after joke and rolled on the ground laughing.

Snake's body was perfect for rolling.

Wolf howl-laughed as he rolled too.

Only Lion stayed at a distance.

"Everyone eats," said Parisa to herself. "And human beings cook."
Parisa boiled a pot of rice. She added pistachio nuts and dried
cranberries to make it fragrant and colorful.

All the creatures came close. Even Lion.

Parisa shivered with fear.

But she took courage from the air, from the sand,
from the water, from the sun.
Nothing could be found without courage, after all.

She put the food in a big wide bowl on the ground.
Because human beings share.
And everyone ate, passing the bowl.

AUTHOR'S NOTE

Dear Reader,

On December 26, 2003, a major earthquake struck the city of Bam in Iran. Half the population died immediately or soon thereafter of injuries sustained in the wreckage. Many children were orphaned.

This book is a fictional tale of a child orphaned by an earthquake. In Farsi, the language of Iran, the name Parisa means "like an angel." The animals in this story are all familiar to Iranian children from Persian folktales and traditional literature. Much of what Parisa says in this story is a gentle allusion to Rumi, a thirteenth-century Persian mystic whose poetry speaks to the modern sensibility as piercingly as ever, and to Iranian poets of today.

ACKNOWLEDGMENTS

Thanks to Eva Furrow, Barry Furrow, David Harrison, Kaveh Mostashari, Parisa Shabani, Richard Tchen, and Jaleh Novini. And a special thank-you to the Iranian writers and translators who advised me, made comments on an earlier version, and generously offered me folktales to work from: Mostafa Rahmandoost, Mohammad Reza Yosefi, Pirouz Ghasemi, and Mohammad Hadi Mohammadi. Thank you to Namrata Tripathi, who encouraged and refined every step. But most of all, thank you to Hossein Ebrahimi (Elvand), without whose guidance and insights this work would not exist.